Bear Tales

Three Treasured Stories

adapted and illustrated by Vlasta van Kampen

Bear and Pig Went to Market

Why Bear Stole the Moon

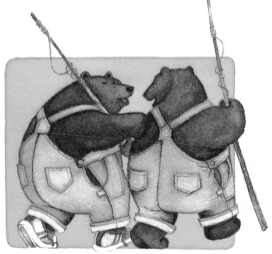

Two Lazy Bears

Annick Press Ltd.   Toronto • New York • Vancouver

Bear and Pig Went to Market

Bear and Pig were best friends. They were always busy planning a new adventure. Since they both loved cooking, they decided it would be fun to start a business selling food. And they did. Bear roasted yummy potatoes and Pig baked delicious sweet buns.

At the local market, they each
rented a stall, set up a stand and
waited eagerly for customers.

While they waited, they dreamed of
all the money they would make
with their fine roasting and baking.

After a short time, Bear became hungry, and Pig's buns smelled so good! He wandered over to his friend's stall.

"How much for a bun?" he asked.

"A nickel," said Pig.

Bear fished in his pocket. He had one nickel, just enough to buy a delicious bun.

Munching away, he lumbered back to his stall to wait for customers.

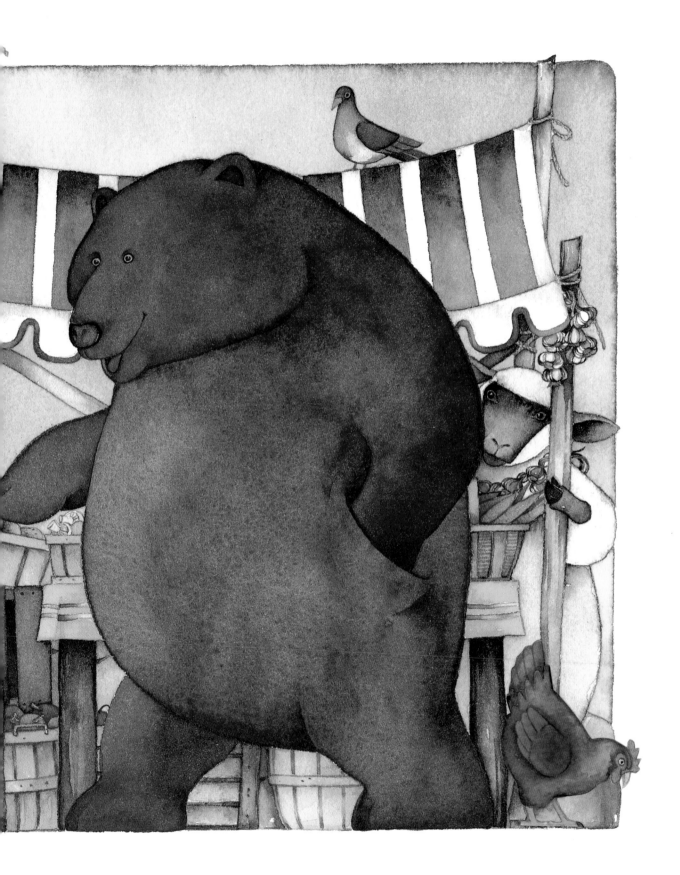

"One sale," thought Pig. "It's a start."

He waited a bit for other customers, but when none came, he strolled over to Bear's stall.

"What delicious-smelling potatoes," remarked Pig. "How much for one?"

"A nickel," replied Bear.

Pig paid Bear, then waddled back to his stall, nibbling on his potato.

Bear was pleased with his first sale, but he was feeling rather hungry again. "Before another customer comes, I should get a bite to eat," he thought.

At Pig's stall he purchased another bun for a nickel.

Not long after, Pig bought another one of Bear's potatoes for a nickel.

Then Bear waited patiently for another customer. No one stopped, so he crossed over to Pig's and bought another bun for a nickel.

Then Pig crossed over and bought another potato for a nickel.

This went on all morning, back and forth, back and forth.

Soon, all the roasted potatoes and sweet buns were gone.

"We should count our money," said Pig.

Bear fished in his pocket and found a nickel. Pig looked in his pocket, but he found nothing. They had sold out—so where was all the money? They double-checked their pockets and still found only one nickel.

"Pig," said Bear, "this is the nickel I started with. It's amazing what best friends can do with just one nickel."

Pig nodded in agreement. "And our food was delicious, too!"
Happily, they headed home to plan another adventure.

Why Bear Stole the Moon

The moon was gone from the great sky. Since it was Raven who knew the night sky, the animals asked him what had become of the moon. Raven told them that Bear had stolen it and tied it in a sack. Bear liked it dark, especially when he hibernated and had his big winter sleep. He would never give back the moon.

But Coyote needed the moon to shine so that he could hunt.

And Raccoon liked the moonlight
to see the fish he'd caught.

Raven wanted to soar in moonlit skies.

And the deer just enjoyed playing in fields bathed in moonlight.

The animals gathered and decided
on a plan to get the moon back.

That evening, they went to visit
Bear. He was a little suspicious but
invited them in, not wanting to seem
unfriendly. After they all got comfy
and cozy, Raccoon began to tell
stories—Bear's favorite bedtime stories.

Soon Bear became very sleepy and
nodded off. The animals scurried about,
looking for the moon. It was quite dark

in Bear's den and hard to see anything.
Coyote noticed a glow under the bed:
it was the moon inside a big sack.

Clever Coyote grabbed the sack,
ran outside and hurled the moon
high up into the sky. It tumbled
and turned, round and round.

Bear woke up and ran outside, crying,
"Moon, moon! Come back! Please don't shine!"

The animals shouted, "Fly, moon. Fly high.
Shine brightly!"

The moon flickered once, twice, then shone
steadily. The animals all cheered, and sad Bear
went back to his cave.

The moon was back in the great sky. Some
nights it is big and round, some nights it is just
a sliver, and some nights it doesn't appear at all.

Two Lazy Bears

Ivan and Igor were two very lazy bears.
AND they argued all the time, from early morning till
late at night.

"Ivan, hang up your clothes," said Igor.

"Why?" asked Ivan. "I need to wear them again. You should tidy up your books," he told Igor.

"Why?" asked Igor. "I might want to read them tomorrow. Why bother?"

"Well then," replied Ivan, "we should at least sweep the floor."

"Why?" asked Igor. "Why sweep it when it gets dirty again!"

So clothes didn't get hung, books didn't get tidied and the floor didn't get swept.

They went fishing instead.

They caught nine fish, but since they were too lazy to carry them home, they gave them to Otter.

All the way home, they argued about what food they would take to the July picnic. It was held every year in the forest.

They returned home tired and hungry, thinking that those fish would have made a lovely dinner. But neither said a word. Ivan chopped wood and Igor cooked supper. They had honey, porridge, and berries for dessert.

All the while they ate, they argued about their plans for the picnic. It was decided that Igor would find a nice big picnic basket and Ivan would bake a cake.

After supper, Ivan pushed his stool back and said, "That was delicious, Igor. I'll just sit by the fire while you clean up."

"Just a minute!" shouted Igor. "I made supper! YOU should clean up."

"But I chopped wood. That was much harder work!" exclaimed Ivan.

"It was not!" Igor shouted back.

"You have to clean up!" said Ivan.

"I do not!"

"You do!"

"I DO NOT!"

"I HAVE AN IDEA!" shouted Ivan. "Let's leave everything until morning. Whoever wakes up FIRST will clean up."

Igor thought this was a good idea, and they lumbered off to bed.

The next morning, both bears lay very still, pretending to be asleep. Neither wanted to be the first one up. Ivan peeked at Igor. Igor peeked at Ivan.

The morning went by. At noon they were both still

pretending to be asleep. The afternoon went by. Ivan had a terrible headache now and Igor was starving.

Just when they couldn't stand it any longer, there was a knock at the door.

Happy for any excuse to get up, they rushed
to see who their visitor might be. It was their
dear friend Goat, who came to see why they
weren't at the picnic that day. THE BIG PICNIC!
By being so silly, they had missed the biggest
event of the year. They had missed all the fun
and delicious food. They decided then and
there not to be so lazy any more.

They made a wonderful breakfast of
pancakes and syrup—even though
it was already suppertime.

This time there was no arguing about cleaning up. Igor swept the floor, and Ivan did the dishes with no fuss at all.

We acknowledge the support of the Canada Council for the Arts, the Ontario Arts Council, and the Government of Canada through the Book Publishing Industry Development Program (BPIDP) for our publishing activities.

Cataloguing in Publication Data

Van Kampen, Vlasta
      Bear tales : three treasured stories

ISBN 1-55037-619-5 (bound) ISBN 1-55037-618-7 (pbk.)

1. Bears – Legends. I. Title.

PS8593.A56B42 2000   j398.24'52978   C99-932362-8
PZ8.1.V4523Be 2000

The art in this book was rendered in watercolors.
The text was typeset in Apollo.

Distributed in Canada by:
Firefly Books Ltd.
3680 Victoria Park Avenue
Willowdale, ON
M2H 3K1

Published in the U.S.A. by Annick Press (U.S.) Ltd.
Distributed in the U.S.A. by:
Firefly Books (U.S.) Inc.
P.O. Box 1338
Ellicott Station
Buffalo, NY 14205

Printed and bound in Canada.

For my son, Dimitri, who
shared his humor, insight and
wonderful creative spirit.
—VvK